Jack and the Aliens

Published in 2013 by Wayland

Wayland
338 Euston Road
London NW1 3BH

Wayland Australia
Level 17/207 Kent Street
Sydney, NSW 2000

Series Editor: Louise John
Cover design: Paul Cherrill
Design: D.R.ink
Consultant: Shirley Bickler

A CIP catalogue record for this book is available from the British Library.

ISBN 9780750259613

Printed in China

This edition published in 2010 by Wayland
Reprinted in 2011 and 2013

Wayland is a division of Hachette Children's Books,
an Hachette UK Company

www.hachette.co.uk

Jack and the Aliens

Written by Andy Blackford
Illustrated by Marijke Van Veldhoven

WAYLAND

Jack was reading a book
about aliens. They visited
Earth in a big silver spaceship.

Everyone was scared of them.

That night, Jack saw a bright light in the sky. He was very excited.

"Dad, Dad! I just saw a flying saucer!" he shouted.

His dad smiled. "I don't think so, Jack. We don't get many aliens around here."

Later, there was a strange green glow in Jack's bedroom. All his toys woke up and started moving about.

At breakfast, Jack told his mum about it.

"The aliens were here last night," he said.

"Oh, Jack, I don't know
where you get these silly
ideas from!" laughed Mum.

Then Mum looked out of the window. There was a big brown circle in the middle of the lawn.

"I wonder what that is," she said. "Dad won't be happy."

"Is this anything to do with you, Jack?" asked Dad.

"No, Dad. I expect it was the aliens," said Jack.

Then there was a knock on
the door. It was the aliens.

"Hi, there!" said Jack. "I was hoping to see you."

The aliens left their shoes
outside. They were very polite.

"We're collecting money for the alien children's hospital," said the blue alien. "Can we wash your car?"

"Dad washed it this morning, thanks," Jack replied. "But maybe you can fix our lawn? Your spaceship burned a hole in it."

The green alien sprinkled
some pink powder on the
grass and it started to
grow again.

"Thank you very much," said Mum, and she gave them a pound.

Later, they got into their spaceship and roared away into the sky.

"Wow!" Jack said. "They were amazing!"

"They were all right," said Dad. "For aliens."

Inside, Jack called for his dog, Fizz, but she didn't come.

"Oh, no!" cried Mum. "I hope
the aliens haven't taken her!"

But Fizz was hiding under the sofa. She didn't come out until dinner time.

"She must have been playing with the aliens," said Jack. "Their powder has turned her pink!"

"It's just one thing after
another in this house!"
said Mum.

"You look cool, Fizz!" laughed Jack. "No one else I know has a pink dog!"

Luckily, Fizz agreed. Being
pink wasn't so bad after all!

START READING is a series of highly enjoyable books for beginner readers. **The books have been carefully graded to match the Book Bands widely used in schools.** This enables readers to be sure they choose books that match their own reading ability.

Look out for the Band colour on the book in our Start Reading logo.

The Bands are:

	Pink Band 1
	Red Band 2
	Yellow Band 3
	Blue Band 4
	Green Band 5
	Orange Band 6
	Turquoise Band 7
	Purple Band 8
	Gold Band 9

START READING books can be read independently or shared with an adult. They promote the enjoyment of reading through satisfying stories supported by fun illustrations.

Andy Blackford used to play guitar in a rock band. Besides books, he writes about running and scuba diving. He has run across the Sahara Desert and dived with tiger sharks. He lives in the country with his wife and daughter, a friendly collie dog and a grumpy cat.

Marijke Van Veldhoven loves to make people laugh. At school she liked drawing cartoons of her friends and teachers that had everyone in hysterics! She lives happily in the Netherlands with her dog and two cats and enjoys long walks.